THE SING-SONG OF OLD MAN KANGAROO

The Sing-song of old man Kangaroo

Rudyard Kipling
Illustrated by Michael C. Taylor

PETER BEDRICK BOOKS
NEW YORK

First American edition published in 1986 by Peter Bedrick Books, New York. Published by agreement with Macmillan Children's Books, a division of Macmillan Publishers Ltd., London and Basingstoke.

Library of Congress Cataloging-in-Publication Data
Kipling, Rudyard, 1865-1936.
   The sing-song of Old Man Kangaroo. (A Just so story / by Rudyard Kipling)
   Summary: Relates how the proud kangaroo became different from all the other animals.
   [1. Kangaroos—Fiction] I. Taylor, Michael C., 1940–
   ill. II. Title. III. Series: Kipling, Rudyard, 1865-1936.
Just so story.
PZ7.K632Si   1986   [E]   85-22920
ISBN 0-87226-073-9

Printed in Hong Kong

10 9 8 7 6 5 4 3 2

THE SING-SONG OF OLD MAN KANGAROO

NOT always was the Kangaroo as now we do behold him, but a Different Animal with four short legs. He was grey and he was woolly, and his pride was inordinate: he danced on an outcrop in the middle of Australia, and he went to the Little God Nqa. He went to Nqa at six before breakfast, saying, 'Make me different from all other animals by five this afternoon.'

Up jumped Nqa from his seat on the sand-flat and shouted, 'Go away!'

He was grey and he was woolly, and his pride was inordinate; he danced on a rock-ledge in the middle of Australia, and he went to the Middle God Nquing.

He went to Nquing at eight after breakfast, saying, 'Make me different from all other animals; make me, also, wonderfully popular by five this afternoon.'

Up jumped Nquing from his burrow in the spinifex and

shouted, 'Go away!'

He was grey and he was woolly, and his pride was inordinate: he danced on a sandbank in the middle of Australia, and he went to the Big God Nqong.

He went to Nqong at ten before dinner-time, saying,

'Make me different from all other animals; make me popular and wonderfully run after by five this afternoon.'

Up jumped Nqong from his bath in the salt-pan and shouted, 'Yes, I will!'

Nqong called Dingo – Yellow-Dog Dingo – always hungry, dusty in the sunshine, and showed him Kangaroo. Nqong said, 'Dingo! Wake up, Dingo! Do you see that gentleman dancing on an ashpit? He wants to be popular and very truly run after. Dingo, make him so!'

Up jumped Dingo – Yellow-Dog Dingo – and said,

'What, *that* cat-rabbit?'

Off ran Dingo – Yellow-Dog Dingo – always hungry, grinning like a coal-scuttle, – ran after Kangaroo.

Off went the proud Kangaroo on his four little legs like a bunny.

This, O Beloved of mine, ends the first part of the tale!

He ran through the desert; he ran through the mountains; he ran through the salt-pans; he ran through the reed-beds; he ran through the blue gums; he ran through the spinifex; he ran till his front legs ached.

He had to!

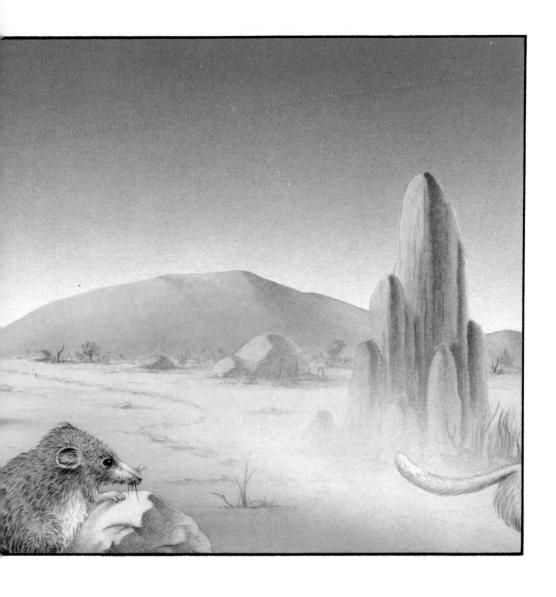

Still ran Dingo – Yellow-Dog Dingo – always hungry, grinning like a rat-trap, never getting nearer, never getting farther, – ran after Kangaroo.

He had to!

Still ran Kangaroo – Old Man Kangaroo. He ran through the ti-trees; he ran through the mulga; he ran through the long grass; he ran through the short grass; he ran through

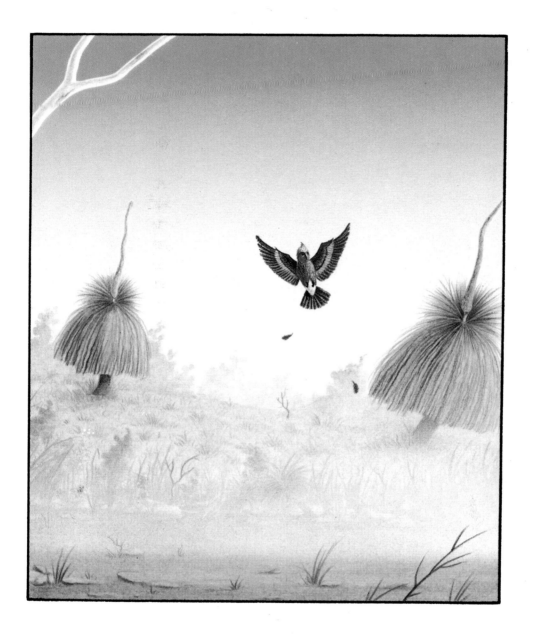

the Tropics of Capricorn and Cancer; he ran till his hind
legs ached.

He had to!

Still ran Dingo – Yellow-Dog Dingo – hungrier and hungrier, grinning like a horse-collar, never getting nearer, never getting farther; and they came to the Wollgong River.

Now, there wasn't any bridge, and there wasn't any ferry-boat, and Kangaroo didn't know how to get over; so he stood on his legs and hopped.

19

He hopped through the Flinders; he hopped through the Cinders; he hopped through the deserts in the middle of Australia. He hopped like a Kangaroo.

First he hopped one yard; then he hopped three yards; then he hopped five yards; his legs growing stronger; his legs growing longer. He hadn't any time for rest or refreshment, and he wanted them very much.

Still ran Dingo – Yellow-Dog Dingo – very much bewildered, very much hungry, and wondering what in the world or out of it made Old Man Kangaroo hop.

For he hopped like a cricket; like a pea in a saucepan; or a
new rubber ball on a nursery floor.
    He had to!

He tucked up his front legs; he hopped on his hind legs; he stuck out his tail for a balance-weight behind him; and he hopped through the Darling Downs.

He had to!

Still ran Dingo – Tired-Dog Dingo – hungrier and hungrier, very much bewildered, and wondering when in the world or out of it would Old Man Kangaroo stop.

Then came Nqong from his bath in the salt-pan, and said, 'It's five o'clock.'

Down sat Dingo – Poor-Dog Dingo – always hungry, dusty in the sunshine; hung out his tongue and howled.

Down sat Kangaroo – Old Man Kangaroo – stuck out his

tail like a milking-stool behind him, and said, 'Thank goodness *that's* finished!'

Then said Nqong, who is always a gentleman, 'Why aren't you grateful to Yellow-Dog Dingo? Why don't you thank him for all he has done for you?'

Then said Kangaroo – Tired Old Kangaroo – 'He's chased me out of the homes of my childhood; he's chased me out of my regular meal-times; he's altered my shape so I'll never get it back; and he's played Old Scratch with my legs.'

Then said Nqong, 'Perhaps I'm mistaken, but didn't you ask me to make you different from all other animals, as well as to make you very truly sought after? And now it is five o'clock.'

'Yes,' said Kangaroo, 'I wish that I hadn't. I thought you would do it by charms and incantations, but this is a practical joke.'

'Joke!' said Nqong, from his bath in the blue gums. 'Say

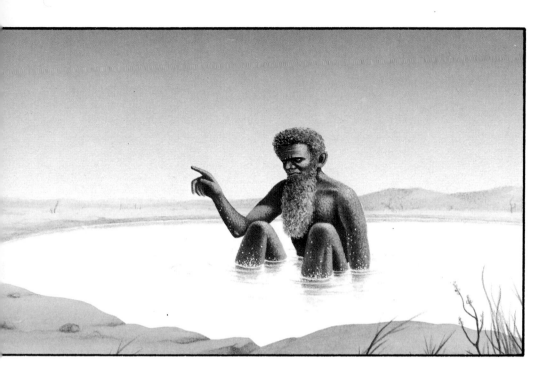

that again and I'll whistle up Dingo and run your hind legs off.'

'No,' said the Kangaroo. 'I must apologise. Legs are legs, and you needn't alter 'em so far as I am concerned. I only meant to explain to Your Lordliness that I've had nothing to eat since morning, and I'm very empty indeed.'

'Yes,' said Dingo – Yellow-Dog Dingo, – 'I am just in the same situation. I've made him different from all other animals; but what may I have for my tea?'

Then said Nqong from his bath in the salt-pan, 'Come and ask me about it to-morrow, because I'm going to wash.'

So they were left in the middle of Australia, Old Man Kangaroo and Yellow-Dog Dingo, and each said, 'That's *your* fault.'

This is the mouth-filling song
Of the race that was run by a Boomer,
Run in a single burst — only event of its kind —
Started by Big God Nqong from Warrigaborrigarooma,
Old Man Kangaroo first: Yellow-Dog Dingo behind.

Kangaroo bounded away,
His back-legs working like pistons —
Bounded from morning till dark,
Twenty-five feet to a bound.
Yellow-Dog Dingo lay
Like a yellow cloud in the distance —
Much too busy to bark.
My! but they covered the ground!

Nobody knows where they went,
Or followed the track that they flew in,
For that Continent
Hadn't been given a name.
They ran thirty degrees,
From Torres Straits to the Leeuwin
(Look at the Atlas, please),
And they ran back as they came.

S'posing you could trot
From Adelaide to the Pacific,
For an afternoon's run —
Half what these gentlemen did —
You would feel rather hot,
But your legs would develop terrific —
Yes, my importunate son,
You'd be a Marvellous Kid!